ox/20

A ROBOT STOLE MY GtRANDMA

For my grandmas Eileen and Mavis. Neither
of whom is or was a robot … as far as I know!
– DC

To Benji, Emma and William with much love x
– CE

STRIPES PUBLISHING LIMITED
An imprint of the Little Tiger Group
1 Coda Studios, 189 Munster Road,
London SW6 6AW

A paperback original
First published in Great Britain in 2020

ISBN: 978-1-78895-182-1

Printed and bound in the UK.

MIX
Paper from
responsible sources
FSC
www.fsc.org   FSC® C020471

The Forest Stewardship Council® (FSC®) is a global, not-for-profit organization
dedicated to the promotion of responsible forest management worldwide.
FSC defines standards based on agreed principles for responsible forest
stewardship that are supported by environmental, social, and economic
stakeholders. To learn more, visit www.fsc.org

10 9 8 7 6 5 4 3 2 1

A ROBOT ATE MY GRANDMA

ILLUSTRATED BY

DAVE COUSINS   CATALINA ECHEVERRI

LITTLE TIGER
LONDON

HAIRY ELEPHANTS
LIKE LAZY ORANGES

"A ROBOT? No way!" The shout came from the group huddled round Brett Burton.

Me and Ali looked at each other. "Uh-oh!" he said as we rushed over.

We were supposed to be rehearsing the school play, *Little Red Riding Hood – The Musical!* Ms Sternwood had written all the songs herself. Unfortunately, the school orchestra (two glockenspiels, three recorders, a tambourine and a triangle) was struggling to bring her musical vision to life. Our head teacher had spent the last five minutes trying to explain that it might sound better if they could at least start and finish the song at the same time … and maybe hit a few of the right notes on the way.

The rest of us had been told to learn our lines, but Brett had got his phone out. He was always finding videos of cats or people doing stupid stuff, but this was different.

The clip showed some glitzy event with a bunch of minor celebrities on a roof terrace somewhere hot. There were fans watching from behind a barrier. Then one of them ducked under it and ran over to get a selfie with the stars. The guy had gone barely three steps when a huge bodyguard grabbed him. But, rather than taking the man back to the crowd, the guard lifted him into the air … then threw him off the roof!

Everyone gasped and Brett laughed. "Don't

worry! He landed in the swimming pool," he said. "But check this out."

The bodyguard had noticed he was being filmed and started walking towards the camera, shouting in a language we didn't understand.

Whoever was filming clearly decided it was time to leave because the picture started jumping around all over the place. But, before the screen went black, the final image was a close-up of the bodyguard's face.

I swallowed.

The man's eyes were glowing bright blue.

"See?" said Brett. "ROBOT!"

Sanjit snorted. "It's fake! They probably put

the glow on afterwards!" But he didn't sound sure.

"Do you think that *was* real?" I whispered to Ali as Brett put his phone away.

My friend shook his head. "Total fake! Real robots don't have glowing blue eyes. We know THAT for a FACT!" He grinned and glanced to the back of the hall where Robin was operating the lights for the play.

Robin is our babysitter. He looks after me and my twin sister Jess while Mum and Dad are at work. Sometimes he helps out at school too. As well as doing the sound and lighting for the play, Ms Sternwood had asked him to be the narrator because he has *such a lovely voice.* In fact Robin sounds just like the posh actor bloke from the satnav Grandma used to make his voice processor.

I should probably explain.

Our grandma is an inventor and Robin IS

actually a robot, but he looks and behaves so much like a real person that most people don't even realize. Ali and my sister's best friend, Ivana, are almost the only ones outside our family who know the truth. We need to keep it that way. Grandma's worried that if people found out what Robin can do, someone could use the technology to make robots that were bad.

But what if somebody already had?

"Jake! Where's your costume?" Ms Sternwood's voice made me jump. "This is a dress rehearsal. Our costumes help us BECOME the character we're playing! How do you expect to BE the rabbit if you're not wearing your ears and fluffy tail?"

Thing is, I didn't *want* to be the stupid rabbit – but our head teacher had insisted that everyone was involved. Ali had managed to get a job helping Robin with the lighting, but they

5

wouldn't let me near anything technical, so I'd been given the role of Third Rabbit.

Dry ice crept across the stage as Red Riding Hood sang and skipped through the cardboard forest to where my sister was waiting.

Jess was the Big Bad Wolf. She says the villain is always more fun to play than the goody-goody hero – especially when that person was Olivia, my sister's arch-nemesis! In the previous scene Jess had *eaten* Grandma and was now sitting in bed dressed as the old lady. Third Rabbit's big moment was approaching and I could feel the nerves crawling up the inside of my furry rabbit onesie.

When Olivia finally reached the end of her song, me and the First and Second Rabbits had to jump out and warn her about the wolf waiting in the cottage. It might not have been so bad if we could have just *told* her, but this was A MUSICAL, which meant there was a whole song-and-dance routine to get through first.

"All of a sudden," said Robin, his voice booming through the speakers, "Little Red Riding Hood came upon a clearing in the forest. It was full of woodland animals playing in the sunshine."

The orchestra stumbled into the opening bars of the song as First Rabbit hopped out and sang, "Don't go to the cottage, Red!"

Rabbit number two joined in with, "There's danger up ahead!"

Then, "Don't go to the cottage, Red!" they sang together.

Which was my cue.

I only had one line in the entire play. I'd been over it a million times. But when I opened my mouth…

It was gone!

My brain was empty. A wordless void.

Everyone was waiting – Olivia glaring at me like she wished her eyes were lasers.

Then Robin's voice sliced through the silence. "Hairy elephants like lazy oranges," he said.

For a moment I wondered if that was the line I was supposed to sing. I saw Ms Sternwood leafing through the script, trying to find the part with elephants...

"Choose a name, you orang-utan umbrella,"
said Robin and somebody laughed.

I was grateful that attention had been taken
off me — until I realized what was happening.
There was something wrong with our robot.
He was malfunctioning.

In school!

IN FRONT OF EVERYONE!

WHAT BIG EARS YOU'VE GOT

"That was too close," I said as we walked out of school later.

"I can't believe Ms Sternwood believed Robin just picked up the wrong script!" My sister shook her head.

"I'm terribly sorry," said the robot. "I don't know what came over me!"

"Don't worry," I told him. "We'll get Grandma to give you a full check-up."

We went home to dump our bags and collect Digby, our dog.

"You're not actually going to *use* that, are you?" Jess pointed to the baby-carrier Robin was strapping to his chest.

Ever since our old teacher, Mrs Badoe, had come into school with her baby in a sling, Robin had wanted one for the dog. I blamed Grandma. When she programmed Robin with information about our family, she forgot to mention that Digby WAS A DOG. As a result, the robot treated him as if he was our exceptionally hairy baby brother. Digby didn't seem to mind.

The bus to Grandma's was busy. Jess found a seat near the back so nobody would know she was with us. I sat across the aisle from our robot.

The old man in the seat next to Robin spotted Digby in the baby-carrier. He leaned over and waggled a finger at the dog. "That's a bonny little one you've got there. Good head of hair! What is it? Boy or girl? I can never tell at that age."

"Hairy elephants like lazy oranges," said Robin and my heart kicked.

"Sorry? I didn't quite catch that."

"Choose a name, you orang-utan umbrella!" said the robot.

"Don't worry," I told the man. "He's talking to me." I gave what I hoped was a smile that said *no need to be alarmed – nothing to see here!* but I could feel the panic rising in my chest. I had to shut Robin up before too many people noticed.

"Huge ears are radical, marmalade elf," said the robot, which was kind of embarrassing because the guy *did* have big ears.

The old man frowned. "Is he all right?"

"Half-eaten lemon pie!" Robin announced to everyone on the bus.

A teenager standing by the stairs was laughing and filming the whole thing on his phone.

"Hairy elephants!" said Robin and more people began to laugh.

Jess was mouthing at me to *DO SOMETHING*, but it was like being back onstage – my mind was blank. I just sat there. Frozen.

The bell dinged to announce the next stop and the old man scrambled to his feet, stumbling in his hurry to get away from the strange, shouty man with the hairy baby.

Jess moved down and slipped into the empty seat, then pretended to fuss over *the baby*. When she was sure nobody was watching, my sister jammed her finger up the robot's nose and held it there for a few seconds. Robin slumped forwards and finally fell silent. I'd been too busy panicking to think of pressing the reset button hidden up Robin's nose! For once I was grateful my sister was around.

The relief didn't last long.

"Is your grandad ill?" The woman in the seat behind was frowning at Robin. "He looks like he's fainted."

"He's just having a nap," said Jess.

The woman leaned over for a closer look.

"Are you sure he's still breathing?"

Of course he wasn't breathing – he's a ROBOT!

"He's fine," Jess told her.

But the woman wouldn't go away. "I'm a nurse," she said. "I think I should take a look at him."

"NO!" Jess gave me a worried glance, but what could *I* do? I silently begged the robot to restart before the nurse grabbed his wrist and found he had no pulse.

Some of the other passengers decided it was time to offer some *really* helpful comments:

You're right, he doesn't look well!

I reckon he's kicked the bucket!

The nurse was leaning over further and reaching for Robin. Any second now she'd realize he was made of metal and rubber, not skin and bone. She'd discover he was a robot

and the kid who was filming would put the clip
on YouTube and then the whole world would
KNOW and then…

"OW!" The nurse jumped back, clutching
her hand. "It bit me!"

For a moment I thought
my sister had taken a chunk
out of the woman, but then
I saw Digby's head poking
out from the baby-carrier.

"Sorry!" said Jess. "He
doesn't like strangers near
Grandad."

Thankfully, Robin chose that moment to
reboot and wake up. He blinked a few times,
looked around, then smiled and reached for
the bell.

"The stop for Grandma's residence is
approaching," he said. "We should prepare to
disembark!"

16

THE CURIOUS INCIDENT
OF THE JAMMIE DODGERS

Grandma spends most of her time in the
garage behind her house, inventing stuff. Her
doorbell has an intercom so she can see
who's at the front door without leaving her
workbench.

"*Hello?*" The voice coming from the tiny
speaker in the wall was distorted and crackly.

"IT'S ME – JESS!" shouted Jess as if her
voice had to make it all the way to the back
garden by itself.

"And me!" I said.

"I thought we wanted her to *open* the door?" Jess laughed so loudly at her own joke we almost missed Grandma's reply.

"*I'm sorry, I can't come to the door right now. Please come back later.*"

I elbowed my sister out of the way and spoke into the microphone. "It's Jake, Grandma! We've brought you some Jammie Dodgers!"

"*I'm sorry, I can't come to the door right now,*" the voice repeated. "*Please come back later.*"

"That's EXACTLY what she said before!" Jess frowned.

"Something's wrong," I said. "There's no way Grandma would ignore Jammie Dodgers!"

"May I suggest that we obtain entry to the premises ourselves?" said Robin, producing Mum's spare key.

We let ourselves in but Grandma's workshop was empty.

"So who was that on the intercom?" I said, feeling the hairs on the back of my neck prickle.

My sister rolled her eyes. "There's one in the bedroom too, dummy! Perhaps Grandma's ill?"

"That would explain why she's off Jammie Dodgers," I said as we ran up the stairs.

Jess knocked on the closed bedroom door. "Grandma? Are you OK?"

My sister turned the handle and we peered

into the room. The curtains were shut, but we could make out a Grandma-shaped lump sitting up in bed.

"*I'm ill!*" The voice floating from the gloom was thin and scratchy. "*Best not come too close, dear!*"

I found myself thinking about the school play – the wolf dressed up as Grandma, waiting in bed for Red Riding Hood! I half expected my sister to tell Grandma, *My, what big ears you've got!* But Jess just asked her what was wrong.

"*I have a very infectious disease*," said Grandma. "*Please stay away!*"

It was hard to see much in the dark, but Grandma definitely didn't sound right. Her voice had a strange crackle to it … as though she was still talking through the intercom.

"Good afternoon, Grandma," said Robin, sliding past us. "May I be permitted to examine you? As you know, my software enables me to perform a full medical diagnostic."

"*Please stay away!*" said Grandma. "*I have a very infectious disease!*"

"I will be perfectly safe," Robin reminded her. "Robots are not affected by human germs."

But, as the robot got closer, Grandma started waving her arms and, when she spoke, her voice had changed to a deep growl. "INTRUDER ALERT!" she shouted – and then the bed erupted.

Blankets billowed into the air as Grandma launched herself at Robin, knocking the robot off his feet. Before we could move, she sprang up and rushed at me and Jess.

My sister (who plays in goal for the school football team) dived out of the way, but I just stood there, staring – unable to look away from the pair of piercing, GLOWING BLUE EYES!

Jess says I screamed, but it was more a shout of surprise – because, whatever was attacking us, it wasn't Grandma.

Then Robin hit it over the head with the antique chamberpot from under the bed.

My sister switched on the light and we stared at the thing lying on the carpet. It was wearing Grandma's dressing gown and a grey

wig, but underneath you could see white
plastic and wires poking through the crack
where Robin had hit it.

"What IS that?" Jess was shaking.

"A robot pretending to be your grandma,"
said Robin.

"But if that Grandma is a robot," I said,
"where's the REAL Grandma?"

23

CHAPTER 4

WHAT IF IT'S NOT NONSENSE?

"What do you mean your grandma got turned into a robot?" Ali was mixing paint and only half listening. We'd gone into school early to help finish the scenery for the play and I was trying to explain what had happened the day before at Grandma's.

"Your grandma is missing?" Ivana looked worried.

Jess sighed. "No, Jake's being overdramatic as usual. Mum says Grandma's just gone off somewhere and forgot to tell anyone. She's done it before. But of course Jake thinks she's been abducted by aliens or something!"

"Why isn't Grandma answering her phone then?" I said.

"She's probably got it on silent or she forgot to take it with her." My sister folded her arms, challenging me to argue.

"So she didn't get turned into a robot?" said Ali.

"Grandma must have *made* the robot for security," Jess told him. "To make people think she was at home. She got burgled a few weeks ago, remember?"

"It had blue eyes," I said. "Just like the one in Brett's video."

Ali stopped stirring to look at me. "Brett's video was faked though." He shrugged. "Lots of *people* have blue eyes – maybe it's the same for robots?"

"See?" Ali flinched when Jess pointed at him. "Even Ali thinks there's nothing to worry about."

"But we still have to find Grandma!" I reminded them. "We need her to have a look at Robin. He went funny again – ON THE BUS!"

Ali winced. "What did he say this time?"

"The same as at the rehearsal," said Jess. "Just nonsense."

"That doesn't make any sense," Ali frowned.

"Isn't that what I just said?"

"No, I mean … with a malfunction, you'd expect random words, but you said it's the same every time."

Ali slapped some paint on to a cardboard tree. "Does that look like tree-colour to you?"

"Perhaps it's not nonsense," said Ivana, adding some yellow to Ali's pot.

"How can 'hairy elephants like lazy oranges' *not* be nonsense?" I asked.

Ivana blushed. "No, you're right."

"That would be a first!" said Jess. "What were you going to say, Ivana?"

"Well … you know our homework project?" she said, adding a leaf to Ali's tree. "The one we have to write about women who inspire us?"

"Yeah, you know, Jake," said Jess. "The one you haven't even started yet!"

Jess was gloating because she'd already written five pages for her project on Fleur Pickles. Ever since the TV celebrity entrepreneur came to our school to sponsor our science club, my sister has been her biggest fan.

"My project is about the women in the

French Resistance," said Ivana. "They used to send messages hidden in normal sentences, like *tomorrow it will be sunny, with a chance of rain at four o'clock.* It would sound like they were just talking about the weather, but really it was a secret communication in code."

"You mean Grandma might be trying to send us a coded message?" My heart was racing suddenly. "She must have activated Robin's remote access, like we did when we rescued him from Mr Burton!"

Jess pulled a face. "Or it could just be a malfunction. Like that time he fell in the swimming pool."

"There's one way to find out," said Ali.

I grinned. "Decode the message!"

"This is impossible!" I threw my pen on to the table in the dinner hall. We'd been trying to decode the message all morning and got nowhere.

Jess laughed. "Admit it, Jake. There is no coded message. It's just a malfunction."

"NO!" said Ali, through a mouthful of crisps. "Remember that time we pretended we were spies, Jake?" He glanced at Ivana. "It was a long time ago. We were only young."

"It was last summer," said Jess. "You were ten!"

Ivana giggled.

Ali turned back to me. "D'you remember though? Your grandma showed us that code. The one where the first letter of each word in the message makes a new word. So for *ALI*, you'd send *alligators like igloos*! Which means *hairy elephants like lazy oranges* would be…"

"H-E-L-L-O!" I said. "The first part spells HELLO!"

Ali grinned. "What did Robin say next?" But

my mind suddenly went blank.

Jess sighed. "*Choose a name, you orang-utan umbrella. Huge ears are radical, marmalade elf.*"

We stared at her and she shrugged. "What? I have a good memory. Unlike *some* people…"

"C–A–N–Y–O–U," said Ivana.

"HEAR ME!" I said. "The message is *Hello, can you hear me?*"

For a moment we just sat there in stunned silence, then Jess started to laugh.

"What?"

"OK – you were right about it being a message, but it's just Grandma messing around. If she was in trouble, she'd have said so. This is more like … a postcard."

Ali looked disappointed, then he grinned. "That does sound like your grandma – going on holiday and sending a coded postcard via robot!"

"But what about the other bit?"

"What other bit?"

"After *marmalade elf*, Robin said something else." I turned to my sister. "You were there! You must have heard it!"

"I was kind of busy stopping Robin from revealing to the whole bus that he was a robot! REMEMBER?"

I pictured myself back on the bus and the confused look on the old man's face when Robin called him an orang-utan umbrella …

but the harder I tried to grab it, the further away the memory drifted. But then…

"LEMON PIE!" I said. "After *marmalade elf,* Robin was going on about LEMON PIE."

"L-P?" said Ivana. "What word starts with LP?"

"Are you sure it wasn't *apple* pie?" asked Ali.

I nodded – but *was* I sure? There were no words that started with LP. I must have misheard.

But there *had* been more to the message… I was sure about that.

ALL THE BETTER
TO EAT YOU WITH

I was at school, rehearsing the play, but for some reason *I* was playing Red Riding Hood! When I reached Grandma's cottage, I saw it wasn't Jess dressed as the wolf, but a ROBOT – a giant metal beast with red eyes and razor-sharp teeth!

Then I heard a voice, echoey and distant, coming from deep inside the robot. *"Jake! Can you hear me?"*

It was Grandma – OUR GRANDMA!

"I'm not on holiday! I've been eaten by this

wolf! Can you get me out?"

I wanted to help her, but what could I do?

And then the giant robot wolf opened its jaws…

And I woke up.

"We need to go back to Grandma's!" I announced at breakfast. I knew what they'd think if I said Grandma had visited me in a dream and said she'd been eaten by a robot wolf, so I didn't mention that.

I'd lain awake for hours after my nightmare, too scared to turn off the light, but I'd used the time to do some thinking. Sending a postcard via robot *was* the kind of thing Grandma would do, but making Robin say nonsense out loud risked exposing him as a robot. She'd only do *that* in an emergency.

I'd thought of something else too.

"You know that robot grandma?" I said, refilling my bowl with Choco Bombs, hoping the sugar might compensate for my lack of sleep. "Well, I was thinking…"

Jess gave a snort.

I ignored her and carried on. "If it's some kind of security robot, it might have recorded everything – like CCTV."

Jess groaned. "What's it going to take for you to accept that Grandma's just gone away somewhere?"

"Proof," I said. "A video of Grandma leaving the house with a suitcase would do."

"What if there is no video?"

I shrugged. "We can have a look around – there might be other clues."

"This is a total waste of time," said Jess as we crossed the playground after school. "I need to work on my project and SOME OF US have lines to learn." My sister stopped and her eyes widened. "WHAT ON EARTH IS HE DOING?"

The usual crowd of parents were waiting

at the gate. They were all staring at the figure crawling along the pavement on its hands and knees, peering through a magnifying glass.

"Is that Robin?" said Ali. "Why's he wearing that weird hat?"

"You're worried about his HAT?" Jess sounded mortified.

"Ah, there you are!" said Robin when he spotted us.

"Smoking is bad for you," said Ivana, pointing to the pipe dangling from Robin's mouth.

"This is merely a prop." The robot stood up. "I'm using it to get into character – as Ms Sternwood suggests."

Ali frowned. "I thought you were just doing tech for the play."

"This isn't for the play. This is—"

"Sherlock Holmes!" I realized. "You're dressed like Sherlock Holmes, the famous detective!"

"Very good, Master Jake! As we're visiting Grandma's house to look for clues, I thought it wise to activate my built-in *detective mode*." Robin waved the magnifying glass.

"You've got a DETECTIVE MODE?" Ali looked impressed.

"But why were you crawling along the pavement?" Ivana asked.

"Ah," said Robin. "I was merely taking the opportunity to test my powers of deduction!"

I glanced down at the cracked concrete.

"What did you find out?"

"My investigations lead me to believe that a dustbin is required in the vicinity of your school gate. I found three discarded crisp packets, two chocolate wrappers and five different flavours of chewing gum."

"Hardly the crime of the century," Jess muttered. "Can we please just go? People are staring."

I was worried that Robin might have another outburst on the bus, but this time the journey passed without incident — although his outfit did attract some funny looks.

We arrived at Grandma's and let ourselves in, then carried RoboGran downstairs and sat it at the kitchen table. The dream was still fresh in my mind and I had an urge to open its mouth to check that our real grandma wasn't trapped inside…

"Do you think you'll be able to get it working again?" I asked as Robin unscrewed a panel in the back of the robot's head.

"Oh, yes. My concern is what might happen when I do." Robin stroked his beard. "This is a security robot. I suspect it might not be pleased to see us."

"You mean it'll attack us again?" Jess took a few steps back.

"That outcome is highly likely," said the robot. "I suggest that you retire to a safe distance while I start her up."

I grabbed Digby and followed Jess to the doorway, which was when I noticed the **AUTOMATIC PORRIDGE MACHINE** poking out from one of Grandma's wellies.

The APM had turned breakfast into a war zone for the two weeks we'd tried to use it. The machine heated the porridge perfectly and it tasted great. The problem was the velocity with which it dispensed your breakfast. We'd destroyed three sets of bowls before Mum gave up and returned it to Grandma. Dad said she should sell it to the army as a weapon, and he'd only been half joking.

"What are you doing?" Jess asked when I picked it up.

I nodded towards RoboGran. "If that thing attacks us again, I want a weapon."

"Huh," said Jess, which was as close as my sister ever got to agreeing with me.

"Ready?" asked Robin.

Robot Grandma's body jerked into life and she stood up. Her eyes snapped open and a piercing beam of blue light swung towards me and Jess like a laser gunsight.

"QUICK!" said Jess, pointing at the porridge machine. **"SHOOT IT!"**

But the APM was still heating up, unable to fire.

"RUN!" said Robin.

It was good advice, but, in our haste to escape, me, Jess and Digby all tried to get through the door at the same time. We ended up in a tangled heap on the floor while the robot advanced.

"Oh, dear!" said Robin. He tried to grab Robot Grandma, but only managed to catch

her dressing gown, which came off in his hand
as she lurched towards us.

Of all the ways my short life could have
ended … to be eaten by a naked robot
version of our grandma was not what I had
imagined.

I closed my eyes and hoped it wouldn't hurt
too much.

CHAPTER 6

MOST UNEXPECTED

"Would you care for some tea?"

I cautiously opened one eye and saw Robot Grandma peering down at us. The blue light had gone from her eyes.

"Perhaps a piece of cake?" she suggested. "Or a biscuit?"

"How interesting," said Robin, covering the robot with Grandma's robe again. "Most unexpected."

Jess disentangled herself and scrambled to her feet. "You mean security robots don't usually offer you tea and biscuits?"

"There's something familiar about this robot," I said as Robin helped me up.

"Because it looks like Grandma, duh!" My sister shook her head. "She probably built it from spare parts left over from Robin too."

"I suppose." But it was more than that. I just couldn't work out what.

"Now we know this robot only wants to kill us with cake," said Jess, "can you find Jake some video of Grandma leaving so we can stop this nonsense and go home?"

"That is my very next task, Miss Jess. However, I'm afraid it may take a little time."

While Robin tried to find some security footage, I decided to have a look around. If I discovered something to prove that Grandma had just gone away, then at least we'd know she was OK. But, if I found evidence that something *had* happened to her, it would show everyone that I wasn't just imagining things. I asked Jess if she wanted to help, but she said she had *better things to do than play detective*, so I took Digby instead.

We started in the front room. Digby raced around, giving everything a thorough sniff.

"Good boy!" I told him.

The dog wagged his tail, then rolled over for a belly rub. I didn't remember Sherlock Holmes having to pause an investigation to give Doctor Watson a tummy tickle, but that was the difference between stories and real life. In books and on TV, clues were always really obvious – a bloody fingerprint or the perfect imprint of a boot in wet mud. I had a feeling that we wouldn't be so lucky. This was just Grandma's house, full of Grandma's things – nothing unusual or missing, except Grandma of course...

Then we heard a strange noise coming from

the kitchen and ran to investigate. "What's going on?"

Jess was laughing. "It's that robot – it keeps doing weird stuff!"

On the other side of the table Robin was bent over RoboGran with a screwdriver in his hand. "Your grandma appears to have used a completely new wiring system for this model," he explained. "I'm having to work through by a process of elimination." He gave the screwdriver a twist and the robot jerked, then started to sing.

"It was trying to dance a minute ago," said Jess.

"Maybe this one?" muttered Robin, reattaching the wire. The robot stopped singing and turned to face him.

"Give us a kiss!" it said.

Jess laughed. "Not that one either then!"

Robin shook his head. "I'm sorry, Master Jake, but I can't find a video recording device anywhere on this robot!"

Jess started to say something about it being a waste of time anyway, but was drowned out by Digby barking at the back door. When I let him out, assuming he needed a wee, the dog ran straight to Grandma's garage.

"You think he's found something?" I said, picking up the Automatic Porridge Machine.

"Probably just a cat," said Jess, following me and Robin across the garden.

When we reached the garage, I hesitated.

I'd been in Grandma's workshop before – it was full of dark, dusty corners where you just know there are going to be the BIGGEST, HAIRIEST spiders you've ever seen.

"Allow me," said Robin, pulling open the door.

We waited while the dusty fluorescent tubes flickered into life, making the shadows dance across Grandma's weird and wonderful creations: the failed **RAPID-WRAP-IT!** from Christmas; a nameless contraption that was part bicycle, part karaoke machine; and the truly terrifying **STYLOMATIC SELF-HAIRSTYLING SYSTEM**, guaranteed to give you the *scare-cut* of your life! There were piles of stuff yet to be transformed too – old engine parts, a lawnmower, a tin bucket full of taps. Threaded through the roof beams were lengths of pipe and silver ducting that looked like they belonged on a spaceship. Digby was

49

staring up at them, a low growl in his throat.

"There's something up there," I muttered.

"I told you," said Jess. "A cat probably got in here."

A cat would be OK. I liked cats. Better than a spider any day.

I pointed the porridge machine at the jumble of junk in the roof and saw a pair of red eyes staring back.

"Um ... do cats have red eyes?"

I checked the gauge. The APM was almost ready to fire. I could smell the porridge heating up.

"It's moving," said Jess. "Robin, what *is* that?"

But, before the robot could answer, the thing dropped from the rafters and pounced at the porridge machine.

Robin flung himself in the way just in time. "Get behind me!" he shouted as the creature scampered across his body. It was long and furry like a cat, but definitely NOT a cat. Robin was fast but this beast was even quicker. It whipped up and down him like a helter-skelter, then disappeared under his Sherlock Holmes hat, reappearing seconds later to glare at us.

And then, from the darkest corner of the garage, came a strange cry.

At first I thought a pile of sheets had come to life, but then I realized it was an old lady wrapped in a million cardigans. She had a large stick in her hand and was rushing towards us.

I didn't mean to shoot her.

I panicked and the APM just went off in my hand.

CHAPTER 7

WEE FREDDIE

"Look what you've done!" Jess knelt beside the body on the ground. It wasn't moving. "I can't believe you shot a poor, defenceless old lady!"

"She wasn't *that* defenceless! Look at the size of that STICK!"

"It's a *walking* stick! All she did was say *hello!*"

"She jumped *out* at me! Anyway it was an accident."

My sister frowned. "Actually, I believe you."

"You do?"

"Yes, because if you'd *meant* to shoot her

you'd have missed!" Jess shook her head.
"What if she's dead?"

"The aged lady is merely unconscious," said
Robin, switching to medical mode.

"What is that THING?" Jess pointed at the
creature that wasn't a cat. It was dancing from
side to side on the old woman's chest, hissing
and showing its teeth. Digby was watching it
warily from a safe distance.

"The animal is a ferret," said Robin.

Which is when the old lady suddenly sat up
and sniffed. "I smell porridge," she said.

"It was him." Jess pointed at me. "He shot
you with the Automatic Porridge Machine!"

The woman nodded. "Aye, that explains
it." She selected a pair of glasses from the
collection hanging around her neck and peered
at us. "Och! Jake and Jessie! You've grown since
I saw you last!" She turned to Robin. "And
who's this handsome fellow?"

"Um, this is Robin," said Jess.

Robin helped the old lady to her feet. "Very pleased to meet you, madam."

"*Madam*, is it!?" She chuckled. "You're a smooth young rascal and no mistake! I'll have to keep ma eye on you."

"Excuse me, but who are you?" My sister folded her arms. "And what were you doing in our grandma's garage?"

"I'm Granny Anderson, you pair of dafties! Your great-granny. I came as soon as I heard."

"Heard what?" I asked.

55

missing!"

...'ma. It was strange

...someone's little

...ss, giving

...old lady was

...she's probably just gone off

...one of her trips."

Granny Anderson shook her head. "Aye,
that's what your ma said when she telephoned
to ask if I'd heard from her, but something's
no right. I can feel it in ma water!" She
scooped up the ferret and draped it round her
shoulders like a scarf. "Enough bletherin'. Now
we're all acquainted, let's get on wi' it."

"Get on with what?" asked Jess.

"Finding your grandma!"

It was good to finally have someone
who agreed with me, but at the same time
there was something a bit … strange about

Granny Anderson.

I'd forgotten about RoboGran until we walked back into the kitchen. I thought Granny Anderson would freak out when the robot offered her tea and biscuits, but the old lady said that *tea and a Jammie Dodger would be lovely.* I wondered if she even realized she was talking to a robot.

"What's that smell?" said Jess, wrinkling her nose.

"I believe the ferret is responsible for the distinctive aroma." Robin gave the creature a doubtful look and Granny Anderson laughed.

"Aye! Wee Freddie does get a bit whiffy when he's stressed. You'll no mind it after a while." She grinned. "That reminds me. Would you grab me something your grandma likes to wear?"

"What's it for?" I asked as my sister returned with Grandma's second favourite scarf.

Granny Anderson placed the ferret on the table. "We're going to use Wee Freddie here to track your grandma."

"I wasn't aware ferrets could do that," said Robin.

"Aye, but Wee Freddie's no ordinary ferret!" The old lady looked at me and winked. "Besides, he's awful fond of your grandma." She fumbled in her pocket and pulled out a collar, wrapping it round the ferret's neck. "We'll never keep up wi' him on foot, but there's a tracker in here."

I wondered why Granny Anderson just happened to have a tracking device in her cardigan, but now didn't seem the time to ask.

"Um, Granny…" Jess looked worried. "I think you might have done his collar up a bit tight. He seems to have passed out!"

"What?" Granny Anderson looked at the ferret dangling from her hand, as limp and lifeless as a wet sock. "Again, Freddie?" She shook her head. "Always falling asleep on the job this one!"

"Can't you just wake him up?" I asked.

"You can try but you'll no get very far. He'll be out for hours now." Granny Anderson draped the sleeping creature back round her neck.

"But we need him to find Grandma!"

"May I suggest we try Digby?" said Robin. "Sherlock Holmes used a dog to track a suspect in one of *his* cases."

"Digby!?" My sister snorted. "THAT Digby?"

Our trusty hound was by the back door, chewing one of Grandma's wellies. He looked up when he felt our eyes on him and wagged his tail.

"Maybe Digby has hidden talents," I said, though deep down I knew that Jess was probably right. Digby's good at stuff like eating, sleeping and weeing up car tyres. I wasn't so sure about his tracking skills. But Granny Anderson thought it was worth a try.

The dog didn't have a clue what was going on, but he wagged his tail again and looked quite alert when Robin held the scarf out. "Find Grandma! Good boy!"

I expected Digby to wander around for a bit, then go back to chewing the welly – instead he ran straight to the front door.

"Here we go," said Granny Anderson. "We'll have your grandma back home eatin' Jammie Dodgers before you know it!"

CHAPTER 8

IS THAT...?

Robin clung to Digby's lead as the dog sped off down the road. Me and Jess had to run to keep up.

"Bet you he takes us straight to the park," said Jess.

But the dog raced on past, his nose glued to the ground.

"He's actually doing it," I panted. "He's following the trail ... leading us to Grandma!"

"Wait! Where's Granny Anderson?" My sister looked behind us, but there was no sign of the old lady.

"She probably couldn't keep up and
decided to wait in the house." I'd barely
finished the sentence when we heard a noise.
It sounded like a really big insect or maybe a
tiny aeroplane. Then something that looked
a lot like a small garden shed on wheels tore

round the corner and hurtled towards us.

"Is that…?" My sister's jaw dropped. "It can't be!"

The garden shed was attached to an ancient motorbike, and as it got closer we could see Granny Anderson crouched low over the handlebars. She was wearing goggles, and the sleeping ferret was still wrapped round her neck. The old lady waved as she sped past, smothering us in a cloud of blue smoke.

"Hang on, this road leads to the back of Grandma's house," said Jess, still coughing as we followed them down a side street. "That daft dog's taken us in a huge loop back to where we started!"

There was a large white SUV with tinted windows parked by the row of garages. Digby ran over and started sniffing the back wheel. Robin tried to pull him away, but the dog REALLY wanted to claim that tyre! Even when the robot picked him up and carried him back into Grandma's garden, Digby was still fighting to get free.

Meanwhile, Granny Anderson had parked her motorbike-and-shed-combination, and now SHE was inspecting the car, her nose about a centimetre from the paintwork. We'd just reached her when the rear window slid down and a woman stuck her head out. "Can I help you?"

My sister squealed. "Fleur Pickles!"

The TV celebrity looked alarmed. A bulky bodyguard in dark glasses jumped out of the vehicle, but then Fleur Pickles peered more closely at us. "Jess and Jake, isn't it?" She smiled and waved the man back into the car.

"You remembered my name!" Jess looked like she was about to faint from happiness.

I could have pointed out that Fleur Pickles had remembered *my* name too – which was surprising given that I'd only met her properly once.

"What are *you* doing here?" I asked.

"Ms Pickles used to live round here," said Jess.

Fleur nodded. "That's right and … well, now my factory's nearby too, so…"

"This is TV Celebrity Fleur Pickles," Jess told Granny Anderson. "She owns her own company. Her products can be found in over

twenty million homes worldwide! I'm doing
her for my project at school about women
who inspire us. In fact, could I have a photo
with you?" My sister pulled out her phone.

"NO PHOTOS!" The car door flew open
again, but Fleur Pickles raised a hand and the
bodyguard got back in.

"I'm sorry, but I don't like having my photo taken." Ms Pickles actually blushed. She nodded towards Grandma's garden. "Is this your house?"

"Our grandma lives here," I said. "Only she's gone missing."

"Gone missing!" Fleur Pickles looked shocked. "How awful. Have you called the police?"

Granny Anderson gave a snort. "The polis! They're about as much good as a chocolate teapot!"

"Only Jake thinks she's missing," said Jess, glaring at me. "Grandma probably just went on holiday and forgot to tell us."

"That does sound more likely. I'm sure she's fine." Fleur Pickles looked genuinely relieved, which was nice considering she didn't even know Grandma.

"We don't know for certain," I said. "That's why we're investigating."

"You are? How ... enterprising of you."

Fleur Pickles frowned and glanced towards the house. "Let me give you my card," she said, smiling again. "Maybe you'd like to have a look around the factory – for your project? Would that make up for not having a photo?"

Jess clutched the card to her heart like it was a golden ticket.

"Ask your parents to give me a call and we'll set something up," said Fleur Pickles. "You can let me know how your 'investigation' is coming along." Then her window slid up and the car drove away.

The moment we got inside Grandma's house, my sister turned on me. "Why did you have to tell her we were *investigating*? It makes us sound like ... children!"

Robin coughed. "Miss Jess," he said. "I feel I should point out that you are, in fact, children."

My sister pulled a face. "Yes, but I'm very mature for my age. Mum says so!"

"Anyway you should thank me," I said. "If we hadn't been here looking for Grandma, you wouldn't have met Fleur Pickles."

"I suppose." My sister's face went all dreamy again. "Who'd have thought we'd meet *Fleur Pickles* ... here!"

She was right. TV Celebrity Fleur Pickles belonged on television or onstage at the science fair, not parked by the garages at the back of Grandma's house...

That's when it hit me. "THAT ROBOT!" I pointed at RoboGran. "It's the one from the science fair. The one Mr Burton built!"

"What?" said Granny Anderson.

I explained how our neighbour, Mr Burton, had built a robot for the science fair where Fleur Pickles was a host. Before it went wrong, the robot had served tea to the judges. *That's* why it seemed so familiar – I'd seen it before!

"But what's Grandma doing with Mr Burton's robot?" said Jess.

The answer seemed so obvious now, I couldn't believe we hadn't thought of it earlier.

"Mr Burton's got Grandma! He left the robot as a decoy, in case anyone came round."

Granny Anderson looked puzzled. "But what would this Burton fella want wi' your gran?"

"He wants to know how to build a better robot! He tried copying Robin but that didn't work, so now he's kidnapped Grandma!"

Too late, I realized what I'd said.

I'd just told Granny Anderson that Robin was a robot.

CHAPTER 9

THE DAFT AULD LADY ROUTINE

"I'm no daft!" Granny Anderson said, chuckling at the look of panic on our faces. "You think I hadn't guessed Handsome here was a robot? Last time your grandma visited, she wouldn't shut up about yon metal man!"

"You can't tell anyone," said Jess. "It has to stay a secret!"

"Don't you worry about me, hen. It's this Burton fella we need to have a wee word with! If he's hurt ma girl…" She left the threat hanging.

"You're sure that's Mr Burton's robot?" Jess looked at Robin and he nodded.

"It would explain why the wiring is unlike your grandma's usual work," he said, peering into the robot's head. "I have also located the science fair demonstration software. There's no doubt that this is his robot."

I could tell Jess was wavering. "But do you really think Mr Burton's got Grandma?"

Robin stroked his beard. "The evidence certainly suggests that he is involved..."

When Granny Anderson offered to drive, I was relieved we wouldn't have to risk the bus again. Thirty seconds into the journey I was having second thoughts.

Robin was on the motorbike with Granny Anderson, but me, Jess and Digby were squashed into the shed-on-wheels. The sidecar felt like it was about to shake itself apart around us and the noise was deafening. But that wasn't the worst part.

I'd already guessed from the pairs of glasses hanging round her neck that Granny Anderson's eyesight wasn't the best. I didn't realize quite how bad until she went through two red traffic lights, and the wrong way round the one-way system. If we hadn't been on a motorbike, we'd never have squeezed past that taxi…

When we finally shuddered to a stop outside our house, Jess leaped from the sidecar and started shouting that Granny Anderson had almost killed us all!

The old lady removed her goggles and grinned. "We've arrived, haven't we? No harm done."

"NO HARM?" Jess was so angry she could barely speak. "That taxi almost ended up in the canal!"

Robots aren't supposed to experience fear, but even Robin looked shaken. "I counted twelve different traffic violations on that journey," he told her.

"Twelve? Is that all? I must be losin' ma touch!" Granny Anderson chuckled, then peered over the fence at Mr Burton's house. "So, that's our target?"

Robin pulled out his magnifying glass and walked over to our neighbour's recycling bins.

"What's he *doing*?" Jess looked horrified.

"I'd say he was lookin' for evidence," said Granny Anderson.

"In the bin?"

"There's many a secret to be found in the things folk throw away," she said as Robin pulled something from the bin and held it aloft with a triumphant cry.

A mouldy teabag didn't seem much of an *Aha!* moment to me, but the robot was excited. "This teabag is your grandma's favourite brand," he said, giving the soggy item a sniff. "Brewed within the last two days!"

"She's here," muttered Granny Anderson turning to me and Jess. "Right! You pair ring his bell and keep him chattin' while me and Sherlock look inside."

"You can't just break in!" said Jess, but Robin and the old lady were already scurrying along the fence in a comical half-crouch with Digby at their heels.

"What are we supposed to say to him?" I asked as we walked round to the front of the house. "Excuse us, but have you kidnapped our grandma?"

My sister raised an eyebrow. "How about I do the talking?"

As Jess reached for the bell, I saw Robin helping Granny Anderson over the fence into Mr Burton's garden.

Our neighbour opened the door wearing a bright yellow Hawaiian shirt and shorts, with grey ankle socks and sandals. "What do YOU want?"

"Have you kidnapped our grandma?"

said Jess.

To be fair, that outfit was enough to make anyone forget what they were supposed to say – or rather NOT say!

"What?" Mr Burton frowned.

"I mean, have you seen Grandma?" My sister's cheeks flushed. "I need to give her a message. Mum said she saw her in your garden earlier. If she's busy, maybe you could pass it on for me?"

Clever, I thought to myself. *If we could get him to admit Grandma was there...* I risked a glance along the side of the house and saw Robin's foot disappearing through a window.

"What nonsense! Why would your grandma be in my garden?" Our neighbour's eyes narrowed. "What are you up to?"

"Nothing," said Jess quickly. "We just thought we saw her and—" A loud crash from the garage cut her off.

"I knew it!" Mr Burton pushed past us, but before he reached the door it swung open and Granny Anderson hobbled out. The old lady was leaning heavily on her stick and looking around with a confused expression.

"What are you doing in my garage?" demanded Mr Burton. "I should have you arrested for trespassing!"

Granny Anderson peered up at him. "Oh, hello, dear! You'll have to excuse a daft wee auld woman, but I seem to have got mysel' lost again! I was lookin' for Jake and... Och, there they are!" She waved and shuffled towards us.

"This is our great-grandma," said Jess. "She's

very old and she gets confused sometimes. This is Mr Burton, Granny."

Our neighbour moved towards the garage where Robin and Digby were searching for Grandma, but Granny Anderson grabbed his hand. "You're the robot man!" she said, pulling him close.

Me and Jess looked at each other. What was she doing?

"Jake's been tellin' me all about you," said Granny Anderson. "I told him *you're pulling ma leg!* But he says *no, Granny, he built himself a robot!* I says *NOOO!* But he says *AYE!*" She paused and leaned closer to whisper, "Could you show me? I've never seen a real robot!"

Our neighbour stared at her, then glanced at us like he suspected it was a trick. But she was just a sweet old lady – what could she possibly be up to?

"I sold it," he said, attempting something close to a smile. "TV Celebrity Fleur Pickles said my robot had great potential. She made me an offer I couldn't refuse."

"Hang on! You sold your robot to Fleur Pickles?" I thought I'd misheard.

Mr Burton smirked. "And now I'm going on a well-earned holiday to the Bahamas!" He spread his arms as if that excused the clothes he was wearing. It didn't.

"He had a robot but he sold it," said Granny Anderson with a sigh. "What a world we live in!" Then she held on to his hand and kept him talking until I saw Robin and Digby climbing back over the fence into our garden.

"I can't believe I let you talk us into that," said Jess when we were all safely back at home.

"It wasn't just me!" I pointed out. "Robin said he thought Mr Burton was involved – and what about the teabag?"

"It was just a teabag!" snapped Jess. "Rubbish – like this whole investigation!"

I looked at the robot. He was covered in cobwebs from Mr Burton's garage and there was a spider dangling from his Sherlock Holmes hat. "You're sure Grandma wasn't there?"

He nodded. "We made a thorough search of the premises, but found no sign of her anywhere."

"What about RoboGran?" I said. "Does nobody else think it's weird that a robot made by Mr Burton, then bought by Fleur Pickles, ended up in Grandma's bed? Seriously, you don't think that's just a tiny bit suspicious?"

Granny Anderson nodded. "Aye, I do!"

"May I suggest a possible explanation?" Robin gave his pipe a thoughtful suck. "Your grandma was worried that somebody would use her technology for evil purposes. If she discovered that Ms Pickles had purchased Mr Burton's robot, it's likely that she would want to buy it back, thus protecting her designs from falling into the wrong hands."

"See?" said Jess. "It's obvious really!"

"But why dress it up to make everyone think she was ill in bed?" I asked.

"So people would think she was at home WHILE SHE WENT ON HOLIDAY!" My sister shook her head. "Grandma said she needed to improve her security after the break-in. She probably thought if she had a spare robot she might as well use it – even if it wasn't as good as Robin."

The robot clapped his hands. "A very logical hypothesis, Miss Jess!"

Jess beamed as if she'd just been given a gold star at school.

I turned to Granny Anderson. "What do you think?"

"I think it's more than a wee bit fishy how yon fancy pants off the telly keeps poppin' up! First round the back of your grandma's house and now this."

"TV Celebrity Fleur Pickles?" Jess looked shocked, then she started to laugh. "You can't seriously think SHE did anything wrong!"

Much as it hurt, I had to agree with my sister. Robin's explanation for RoboGran made sense. It was only me and Granny Anderson who thought that something *had* happened to Grandma – and we had no actual evidence, just a feeling. But that was the problem.

I wished I could let it go and accept that Grandma had gone on holiday, but the feeling that something wasn't right … it wouldn't go away.

CHAPTER 10

GREETINGS FROM BOGNOR REGIS

"I told you there was nothing to worry about!" Mum smiled as we passed the postcard round the table at breakfast the next morning.

There was a photo on the front showing a sandy beach and a pier, with people walking along the promenade. On the back was a message from Grandma.

Greetings from Bognor Regis! Thought I'd treat myself to a few days at the seaside. Might have forgotten to tell you I was going! Sorry. See you all soon. Love Grandma xx

Jess handed it to me with an *I told you so!* look on her face.

I tried to be happy that Grandma was OK, but I knew Jess was never going to let me forget this. And there was still that nagging feeling that something was wrong – but how could there be? The postcard was proof.

"I suppose your great-granny will go back to Scotland now," said Mum, glancing towards the ceiling. Granny Anderson was still asleep upstairs – we could hear her snoring. "It's been nice to see her, though I won't be sorry to say goodbye to that ferret."

"Yeah," said Jess. "I didn't think anything could smell worse than Jake!"

I ignored her and took my bowl to the sink where Robin was looking at the postcard through his magnifying glass.

"What's wrong?" I asked, thinking Robin must still have suspicions too.

86

The robot handed
me the magnifier
and pointed. "Look!
There on the pier.
That dog looks just
like Digby!"

Or maybe not.
Robin's detective mode was
clearly no longer in operation.

Ms Sternwood clapped her hands for
attention. "This is our last rehearsal before the
performance tomorrow evening. You should all
know your lines by now, so no scripts allowed."

I sighed and tugged at my costume. "This
thing really rides up," I muttered to Ali.

"Jake, please don't do that onstage in front
of the parents," said Ms Sternwood.

I blushed and took my position among the

trees, then checked that my one line – *That's not Grandma in bed* – was still written on the back of my hand. I didn't trust myself not to panic and go blank again.

The words made me think about the robot we'd found in Grandma's bed. Robin had come up with a reasonable explanation for that, and the postcard proved that Grandma had just gone on holiday. So why was I still thinking about it?

"JAKE!"

When I looked up, everyone was staring at me. I must have missed my cue.

I hopped forwards and looked at the words on the back of my hand. "That's not Grandma in bed!" I blurted – then realized, too late, that there was no music playing and Olivia hadn't started to skip through the forest yet.

When the laughter died down, Ms Sternwood sent me to the toilet to wash the words off my hand. Ali came with me.

"At least you got your line right," he said. Then, "Ew! Someone's dropped a half-eaten Mars Bar down the toilet. It looks just like a—"

Suddenly I was back on the bus with Robin...

"Half-eaten!" I said.

"Yeah, what a waste!"

"No!" I grabbed Ali's arm. "That's what Robin said! HALF-EATEN LEMON PIE – that was the rest of the message!"

Ali's eyes widened. "HELP!"

"What's the matter?"

"NO!" he said. "*Half-eaten lemon pie. It spells H–E–L–P!*"

"So Grandma's message was: *Hello, can you hear me? Help!*" An icy chill trickled down my spine.

"But I thought you said you got a postcard from her this morning?"

"We did." The image from the bus faded. "You're right – the postcard said she was fine. I must have dreamed the lemon pie bit!"

The robot wolf wasn't the only nightmare I'd had recently, and my dreams felt as real as everything else. "It's this stupid play," I said. "It's messing with my head."

Ali laughed. "Don't worry, it'll all be over tomorrow night."

I nodded, but tomorrow night seemed like a long way away. A lot could happen between then and now.

"Hey! We're going for that tour round the Pickle Factory in the morning!" Ali reminded me. "That's something to look forward to."

As promised, TV Celebrity Fleur Pickles
had arranged for Jess, me and two friends to
visit her factory on Saturday morning. Ali and
Ivana were almost as excited as my sister, but I
couldn't stop thinking what Granny Anderson
had said about Fleur Pickles being involved.

"Ready?" asked Ali.

I dried my hands then glanced in the mirror.
A rabbit with floppy ears and wonky whiskers
stared back at me. Maybe it was time to forget
all this nonsense and just *be* the rabbit?

But, as I took my place onstage, the image
of Robin on the bus refused to go away and
I could hear the robot calling out *half-eaten
lemon pie* like he was shouting orders in a café.

PURPLE IGLOOS AND
AVOCADO PENGUINS

I woke up needing the toilet. I tried to ignore
it and lay in the dark, listening to my family's
snores rumbling across the landing. Then
another sound caught my attention. It was
Robin's voice coming from downstairs ... but
who was he talking to?

Suddenly I realized what was happening and
jumped out of bed, praying I'd make it in time.

"Huge ears are radical, marmalade elf," said
the robot as I skidded into the moonlit kitchen.
"Half-eaten lemon pie."

That IS what he'd said! I hadn't dreamed it!

Robin was sitting in his chair by Digby's bed, plugged in to recharge. His eyes were closed like he was talking in his sleep. "Purple igloos can kill lazy ear slugs," he said, which was new. That meant there was more to the message! I had to write it down so this time I wouldn't forget.

"Calvin's avocado penguin telephone," said the robot as I grabbed a pen and scrawled *purple igloos can kill lazy ear slugs* on my arm. "Is very expensive," he told me, so I wrote that next to it.

But what had he said before that?
Something about an *avocado telephone* …
Calvin's avocado telephone … is very expensive.
That was it!

C–A–T–I–V–E. I frowned. Was that a
word?

No, but CAPTIVE was! Calvin had an
avocado *penguin* telephone.

Was Grandma telling us she was being held
captive?!

I waited to see if Robin was going to say
more, but the robot stayed silent.

I switched on the light and read the rest of
the words written on my arm. *Purple igloos can
kill lazy ear slugs.*

P–I–C–K–L–E–S.

As in … Fleur PICKLES?

Jess had laughed when Granny Anderson
suggested the TV celebrity might be involved.
But here she was again…

The full message read: *Hello, can you hear me? Help! Pickles. Captive.*

I stared at the words.

Everything seemed to be leading us to Fleur Pickles, but WHY would she be holding Grandma captive? It made no sense.

I didn't hear Granny Anderson come in and nearly jumped out of my pyjamas when she spoke. "I couldnae sleep either. Thought I'd make mysel' a cup of tea." She nodded towards the ink on my arms. "Paper shortage, is there?"

I hesitated then told her about the message.

"I knew there was something fishy about that fancy pants off the TV!" she said.

"But what about the postcard?"

She snorted. "Anyone can send a postcard."

"But who would do that – pretending to be Grandma?"

"Somebody who wants us to BELIEVE she's away on holiday." Granny Anderson's eyes narrowed. "The same someone who planted that robot in her bed."

The robot Fleur Pickles had bought from Mr Burton…

I remembered Jess telling Fleur Pickles that we thought Grandma had gone on holiday – how relieved she'd looked when we told her that we hadn't called the police.

"But TV CELEBRITY FLEUR PICKLES?" I said. "That's impossible!"

Granny Anderson gave me a strange look. "People aren't always what they seem, Jake. You'd do well to remember that."

That made me think of Little Red Riding Hood… Was Fleur Pickles the wolf? Had she *eaten* our grandma?

I shook my head. What was I on about?

"I must have heard Robin wrong," I said, pulling my sleeve down to cover the words. "It happened really fast."

"Now why'd you think that?"

"Because I'm *always* getting stuff wrong!"

"We all make mistakes, Jake. We're meant to learn from them, no give up!"

The old lady watched me as she dunked a biscuit in her tea.

"You're like me, Jake – you can tell when something's no right, when someone's lyin'. You feel it in your water!" She grinned. "You just need to learn to trust what your instincts are tellin' you. If you don't believe in yourself, how you expectin' anyone else to believe in you?"

But who was going to believe that TV Celebrity Fleur Pickles was holding Grandma captive? Even if all the evidence *did* point to Fleur, I had no actual proof. The word PICKLES could mean anything. Not so long ago I'd been convinced that Mr Burton had kidnapped Grandma, but I was wrong about that. What if I was getting carried away again?

"Are you no forgettin' something?" said Granny Anderson, taking a loud slurp of tea.

"Probably."

She laughed. "I thought you and Jess were off to her factory today?"

I looked at the clock. It was Saturday already. We'd be at the Pickle Factory in just a few hours' time.

"Seems like a perfect opportunity for a rescue to me!" Granny Anderson grinned.

"But Jess is never going to believe that Fleur Pickles is involved! I doubt Ali and Ivana will either."

"So don't tell them. Let Jess go and do her interview – keep Fancy Pants busy while you rescue your grandma!"

"I can't do it on my own!"

The old lady smiled. "Ah, well, I might just be able to help you there."

CHAPTER 12

THE PICKLE
FACTORY

"What IS that smell?" My sister glared at me
accusingly.

Me, Jess and Ali were squeezed into the
back of Ivana's dad's car on our way to the
Pickle Factory. Even with the windows down,
the aroma was getting worse.

Granny Anderson had convinced me it
would be OK.

"We'll stuff Wee Freddie up your jumper,"
she'd said.

"Nobody'll know," she'd said.

What she *hadn't* said was how much the ferret would stink and wriggle about!

Once I'd smuggled Wee Freddie inside the factory, the plan was to release him. "If your grandma's there, he'll find her," Granny Anderson had told me.

It had been exciting, plotting in secret round the kitchen table in the middle of the night. I'd felt quite brave – heroic almost. But now that I was on my way, with an actual ferret stuffed up my jumper, the whole thing seemed a lot less heroic and a lot more likely to get me into loads of trouble.

I wished I'd told Ali what I was doing, but I'd left it too late. By the time we arrived at the Pickle Factory, I felt sick with nerves. Then I saw the security guard in reception checking bags and patting people down.

"Jake? Are you coming?" Ali and the others were waiting.

Wee Freddie chose this moment to readjust his position under my jumper. The thing is I'm ticklish. It was all I could do not to shriek with laughter. Keeping still was impossible – which was lucky because it made it look like the movement inside my hoodie was caused by me dancing around.

"Stop it!" hissed Jess.

But I couldn't. "I need a wee!" It was the first thing that came into my head.

"What's wrong with him?" said the security guard as I danced towards her.

"He needs the toilet," Ali explained.

"Better get you through first then! Don't want any accidents, do we?" Her laugh faded when I stepped up and the full force of stinky ferret hit her. "Just go through," she said, without even attempting to pat me down. "If we're not already too late…"

And, just like that, I was inside. I ran to the toilet and locked myself in a cubicle.

Granny Anderson had told me to release the ferret into the air ducts or roof space. I balanced on the toilet and tried the ceiling tiles – they were loose. Wee Freddie couldn't wait to climb up and scamper into the darkness.

"No sleeping on the job!" I whispered after him. "Find Grandma!"

I replaced the panel then joined the others. I'd done it! And I did feel kind of heroic. Even if it was just relief.

We took the lift to the fifth floor where TV Celebrity Fleur Pickles was waiting in an office that was bigger than our house.

"Have you heard from your grandma?" she asked, sinking back into a large leather chair.

"We got a postcard," said Jess.

"Wonderful! I told you there was nothing to worry about."

That's when I *knew* Fleur Pickles had sent the postcard – I could see it in her eyes.

I had an urge to stand up and demand to know where she was holding Grandma, but I stayed quiet. Granny Anderson and Robin would be outside in the shed-on-wheels, tracking Wee Freddie. When the ferret found Grandma, they'd call me with the location and we could go and rescue her.

"Shall we start with the interview and then do the tour?" Fleur suggested.

Jess nodded. She'd prepared a billion and one

questions to ask, and I realized I should have sneaked a couple of mine in – why Ms Pickles had kidnapped our grandma, for instance!

It was boring just sitting there, listening to Jess drone on, so I looked out of the huge window behind Fleur Pickles' desk. We were on the fifth floor and you could see right across town. I was trying to spot our house when something caught my attention on the other side of the glass.

It was a slipper...

Two slippers ... and a pair of legs in woolly tights.

"Jake?" Fleur Pickles was looking at me. "Are you all right?"

I nodded and tried to keep the shock from my face as the rest of Granny Anderson dropped into view and gave me a thumbs up through the window.

Jess was busy making notes, but Ali and Ivana had both spotted the old lady. Fleur Pickles saw the look of surprise on their faces and spun round in her chair—

Just as Granny Anderson swung out of sight.

Ivana blinked. "There was—"

"A BIRD!" said Ali. "A really … weird-looking one."

Fleur Pickles frowned at the empty sky, then turned back.

"Um, Ms Pickles?" I raised my hand. "Is there a toilet nearby?"

"I think I need to go as well," said Ali.

The moment we were outside the room he grabbed my arm. "TELL ME YOU SAW THAT!"

"She went this way," I said, trying the door of the room next to Fleur's office.

It opened on to a large storeroom with stacks of shipping crates and giant rolls of bubble wrap. Granny Anderson was standing by an open window.

"Slight change o' plan," she said, shrugging off her climbing harness.

"You just…" said Ali.

"Through the window, aye." Granny Anderson adjusted her cardigans and Digby poked his head out. "This building has some kind of shieldin'," she told us. "It was blockin' the signal from Wee Freddie's tracker, so I had to come in."

She pulled back her sleeve and peered at a tiny screen strapped to her wrist. "That's better."

"Where's Robin?" I asked, half expecting the robot to come crashing SWAT style through the window at any moment.

"I told him to stay wi' the bike and wait for ma signal."

Ali stared at us. "Could somebody please tell me WHAT IS GOING ON!"

I explained as quickly as I could.

"Why didn't you tell me?" Ali sounded disappointed.

"I didn't think you'd believe me."

"I'm your best friend," said Ali. "I always believe you … well, mostly. That time you thought aliens were running the chip shop…" He laughed. *"Classic Jake!* I wasn't so sure about that!"

Granny Anderson walked over to a nearby crate labelled FAULTY. NOT FOR SHIPPING and lifted the lid.

Ali jumped when he saw what was inside. "No way! That's…"

"Exactly like the robot from Brett's video!" I nodded. "Not fake then."

Ali shook his head. "No wonder they're all marked as faulty."

"That's why she needed Grandma!"

Suddenly it all fell into place.

"Fleur Pickles is building robots," I said. "Except they don't work properly—"

"And she needed an expert to fix 'em," said Granny Anderson.

"So she kidnapped your grandma!" Ali's eyes boggled.

"Because Grandma would never help with something like that unless she was forced to!" I pointed at the stacks of crates. "This is exactly what Grandma warned us about. Somebody making a load of bad robots and unleashing them on the world!"

It sounded ridiculous, but at the same time it explained everything.

"What are we going to do?" Ali looked worried.

"For now, you boys had better skedaddle before you're missed," said Granny Anderson. "I've got a ferret to follow! We can save the world later."

"We were about to send out a search party," said Fleur Pickles when we got back. She laughed, but her eyes didn't join in. "I was just telling Jess and Ivana that I'm about to announce my latest Pickles product."

"What is it?" asked Ali.

Fleur Pickles smiled. "I'm afraid that has to stay a secret until the official announcement. What I *can* tell you is that this product will revolutionize our lives. This time next year, there could be one in every home!"

Me and Ali exchanged a look. It was worse

than we'd feared.

Just then there was a knock on the door. A woman came in and whispered something in Fleur Pickles' ear.

"Would you excuse me for a moment," she said, standing up. "There's something I have to deal with."

The second the door closed behind her, Ali turned to me. "You think they've found Granny Anderson?"

"Was that really her outside the window?" said Ivana.

"What?" Jess stared at her friend in disbelief.

Before I could stop him, Ali told them everything.

It took a while and my sister did not take the news well.

"You're ridiculous," she said. "Even if Ms Pickles is making robots, it doesn't mean she's got Grandma!"

"Did someone say my name?"

I swear my heart actually stopped.

When I turned round, Grandma was standing in the doorway.

SURPRISE!

"Look who I found!" said Fleur Pickles, her celebrity smile on full beam.

Seeing Grandma – standing there like that – was a shock. Even Jess looked surprised.

We ran over and gave Grandma a hug and, I'll admit, I gave her an extra squeeze just to make sure she wasn't another robot.

"Your grandma has been working on that top-secret project I was telling you about," said Fleur. "That's why we couldn't tell anybody. I'm sorry if you were worried."

We were all still hugging and smiling, but something didn't feel right.

When the alarm went off, for a moment I thought it was in my head!

"I'm afraid that's the fire alarm!" Ms Pickles had to shout over the din. "I'm sure there's nothing to worry about, but if you could all make your way to the exit!"

"Come on," said Grandma, leading us towards the stairs. But the moment Fleur Pickles was out of sight, she stopped. "We have a problem."

"You mean apart from the building being

on fire?" said Ali.

"There isn't a fire," I told him. "It's probably Granny Anderson creating a diversion!"

"My mum's here?" It was Grandma's turn to look surprised.

"Long story," I said as we clanged down the metal stairs. "We got your message and thought you needed rescuing."

"I told you it was rubbish!" The gloating in my sister's voice was so loud I could hear it over the fire bell.

"Actually, it wasn't," said Grandma. "I'm sorry, Jess. I know you think the world of Fleur Pickles, but I'm afraid she's not quite what she seems."

"What d'you mean?"

"She's building robots, Jess. Bad robots." The alarm stopped and Grandma's words left an ominous echo in the silence. "Sometimes good people are corrupted by success and power.

They get carried away with it and—"

"Build a robot army to take over the world!" said Ali.

"But you were helping her!"

Grandma shook her head. "She gave me no choice, made all kinds of threats, so I pretended to help. I fixed a couple of small things so she would trust me, then programmed a virus into the robots' software. Unfortunately I didn't have time to activate it before Fleur let me go."

"Why did she let you go?" I asked.

"That's what I wanted to tell you." Grandma turned to face us. "Fleur Pickles let me go because she doesn't need me any more – not now she's got Robin!"

"WHAT?" I stared at her.

"Apparently they caught him trying to break in."

"But he was supposed to wait outside!"

Grandma sighed. "Robin must have thought you and Jess were in danger. He's programmed to protect you. That overrules every other instruction."

"We need to get him back," said Jess in a menacing growl.

I nodded. I was surprised how good it felt to be on the same side as my sister again.

"I know where she'll have taken him," said Grandma. "Follow me."

We'd barely gone ten steps when something crashed through the ceiling and pounced on Grandma. Someone screamed – I think it was Ali.

"Wee Freddie!" said Grandma as the ferret wrapped himself round her neck and nuzzled under her chin.

"He did it!" I laughed. "He found her!" For all Granny Anderson's claims that Wee Freddie was no ordinary ferret, I was still impressed.

Then something else loomed into view ahead of us. The thing appeared to have two heads and what looked like a large weapon in its hand. Was this a different, even scarier robot Fleur Pickles was building?

Then one of the heads detached itself and ran towards us.

"Digby!" said Ivana.

"Is that my Automatic Porridge Machine?" said Grandma.

"Och! Ma wee lassie!" Granny Anderson dropped the APM and pulled Grandma to her chest. "I knew Wee Freddie would find you!"

After much hugging and licking of faces (Wee Freddie and Digby ... mostly!), we told

Granny Anderson about Robin. The old lady's expression darkened and she picked up the porridge machine.

"Right," she said. "It's time Lady Fancy Pants learned what happens when you mess wi' ma family!"

Fleur Pickles' secret lab was deep underground. There was an armed guard outside the door.

"Leave this to me," said Granny Anderson, handing the APM to Jess.

The man seemed surprised to see an old lady hobbling towards him with a stick. "Excuse me, madam!" he said. "This area is restricted."

"What's that, son? You'll have to speak up. Ma hearin's no what it was."

"YOU NEED TO LEAVE," he told her.

"I need the lav, aye!" Granny Anderson reached for the door. "Through here, is it?"

As the guard moved to stop her, there was a blur of cardigans and the thud of a stick. The next moment the man was unconscious on the ground.

"Did you SEE that?" Ali's mouth hung open in pure admiration.

Robot-Stealing-Grandma-Kidnapper Fleur Pickles looked up from her screen when we burst through the door. Robin's head was on the table next to her, wires connecting it to the computer.

Ivana gasped. "What have you done to him?"

"He's quite remarkable," said Fleur Pickles, ignoring the question. "This software is revolutionary. My robots will be invincible once this has been uploaded to their systems!"

Despite his head being disconnected from his body, Robin was still functioning.

"Hello, everyone!" he said. "I'm terribly sorry, but I seem to have got myself captured and dismantled again."

"Don't fret, metal man," said Granny Anderson. "We're here to get you home."

Fleur Pickles laughed an Evil Genius Laugh. "You know I can't possibly allow that."

"And how exactly are you going to stop us, hen?"

"Allow me to demonstrate," said Fleur as the wall of the lab gave an ominous clunk, then started to open like a pair of curtains. "These are my Guardians! The future of personal and home security."

Four robots, just like the one we'd found in the crate, stepped forwards, their heavy boots thumping against the floor.

"Help!" squeaked Ali as the nearest Guardian fixed its glowing blue eyes on us.

"INTRUDERS DETECTED," it said in the kind of voice you didn't argue with. "RESISTANCE IS FUTILE."

Granny Anderson hobbled towards it on her stick. "Hello, young man!"

I grinned. I couldn't wait to see the look on Fleur Pickles' face when her scary robot got destroyed by an old lady!

But, when Granny Anderson tried to repeat the trick she'd used on the guard outside, the robot saw it coming. It dodged the attack, then grabbed the stick with one hand and Granny Anderson with the other.

"My human guards might fall for the old-lady routine, but not my robots!" said Fleur as Granny Anderson was dragged away and locked in a cupboard.

"LET HER GO!"

Even Fleur Pickles seemed surprised by the menace in my sister's voice. Then she saw the Automatic Porridge Machine Jess was pointing at her.

"Jessica! I'm disappointed. I thought you understood the important work I'm doing here."

"You mean kidnapping people's grandmas and stealing robots?"

Fleur Pickles frowned. "I didn't KIDNAP anyone! Your grandma just needed a little … persuasion before she agreed to help."

"So you kept her here as your prisoner?"

"I couldn't let her leave, could I? What if she'd told somebody what we were doing? But it wasn't kidnapping. Your grandma has been very well looked after. Do you know how many packets of Jammie Dodgers I've had to buy?"

"I DON'T CARE!" my sister shouted. "Do YOU know how long it takes to write a thirteen-page, full-colour project?"

Fleur Pickles looked confused.

"A LONG TIME!" said Jess. "And then to find out it's all been a waste, because the person you thought was a hero is actually EVIL!"

124

"Evil's a little harsh, don't you think?"

"No," said Jess and pulled the trigger.

RESISTANCE IS FUTILE

Fleur Pickles' Guardians rushed to form a protective wall against the hail of hot porridge. I'd seen the APM shatter breakfast bowls to dust, but the robots shrugged it off like a light shower of rain.

Then Jess announced she was out of porridge.

"SQUAD, ENGAGE!" shouted Fleur from under the table. "MAXIMUM FORCE!"

"I think you just made them angry," said Ali as the dripping robots lumbered towards us.

"I need to activate the virus to stop them," whispered Grandma. "Think you can distract the robots while I get to a computer?"

I nodded, but I didn't have a clue how – unless running away counted as a distraction?

"Perhaps we can use the tables?" said Ivana.

The lab was like a classroom with rows of desks, and the robots had to walk round them to reach us.

Fleur Pickles watched with amusement as we dragged the furniture until we had the Guardians boxed in like sheep in a pen. She didn't look so happy when Digby jumped on to the table next to Robin's head and started growling at her. At least he was trying – Wee Freddie had climbed back inside my hoodie and gone to sleep.

While all this was happening, Grandma sneaked round to a computer on the opposite side of the room and started typing. So far

Fleur Pickles had been too busy keeping an eye on Digby to notice.

For a few seconds I thought we'd done it.

Then the sound of splintering wood shattered my hopes. Ivana gasped as one of the robots picked up a desk and tore it in half like it was made of paper. In thirty seconds our barricade was reduced to a pile of sawdust and twisted metal.

"You see?" said Fleur Pickles, looking relieved as a robot dragged Digby away from her. "My Guardians are invincible." She pointed at Grandma. "Get her away from that computer!"

I hoped Grandma had already managed to activate the virus, but, as the robot bundled her into the cupboard with Granny Anderson, she looked over and shook her head.

"Did you really think you could defeat me?" Fleur Pickles laughed. "I'm TV Celebrity Fleur Pickles. I'm rich, famous and powerful. I have an army of robots at my command. What do you have? Four children, a filthy dog and two old grannies!"

She sighed then clicked her fingers. "Round them up and throw them in the cupboard with the others!" The Guardians turned their blue gaze towards us.

"Uh-oh!" said Ali and Ivana grabbed his hand.

"If only I had my body!" Robin's head was rocking from side to side with frustration. "It's my job to protect you and I've failed!"

I was about to tell Robin that it wasn't his fault when I realized he'd given me an idea. It was crazy and ridiculous. The kind of idea to make Jess roll her eyes and Ivana giggle – what Ali would have called *Classic Jake!* But at the same time something told me it might just work – I could feel it in my water.

Robin had reminded me that robots have a primary function that overrules all other commands – his was to look after me and Jess.

I remembered how the Guardians had jumped in the way when Jess fired the porridge at Ms Pickles. Did that mean that their most important job was to protect her? If so … maybe if we threatened Fleur the robots would have to help her instead of chasing after us. It might just buy us enough time to get

Grandma and Granny Anderson out of that cupboard.

The problem was how could *we* threaten Fleur Pickles? Like she said, we were just four unarmed kids.

"Get off me, you tin-can tyrant!" Jess shouted as one of the robots grabbed her.

Ivana tried to push the Guardian away, but it was like trying to knock down a brick wall with a balloon.

"Leave her alone!" cried Ali as a second robot lifted Ivana into the air.

I had to do *something*. Once they got me and Ali, it would be game over.

Then I had another idea, even more ludicrous than the first. But Granny Anderson had told me I needed to trust my instincts and believe in myself… Stupid idea or not, this was our only hope.

"Jake! Watch out!" Robin's warning came

just in time.

I ducked as a Guardian lunged, missing me by millimetres. Digby jumped on its back, giving me the precious seconds I needed to get to Fleur.

"Ms Pickles," I said, doing my best Jess impression, "I love you! I'm your biggest fan!"

Fleur Pickles looked up, startled.

"Jake! What are you doing?" I could hear the disbelief in my sister's voice from across the room.

Fleur Pickles smirked. "Yes, Jake. What ARE you doing?"

I'd remembered that meeting by the garages outside Grandma's…

I leaned closer and pulled out my phone. "How about a photo?"

The robot dragging Ali towards the cupboard stopped. "NO PHOTOGRAPHS!" it bellowed.

"Smile!" I told Fleur … and pressed the button.

The Guardian threw Ali to one side and rushed towards me instead – just as I'd hoped. It was only then that I wondered if I should have thought more about what was likely to happen next. At least there wasn't a roof it could throw me off.

I braced myself as metal fingers clamped

round my arm, but then something else happened. It might sound strange to say I'd forgotten there was a ferret up my jumper, but I was as surprised as anyone when Wee Freddie popped his head out and pounced on Fleur Pickles. The TV Celebrity Turned Evil Genius screamed as the ferret dashed across her shoulders … and then the smell hit – much worse than in the car.

"I believe the ferret has sprayed," said Robin, watching from his position on the table. "It is a technique they use to disable an enemy."

The scream worked like a giant magnet. Every robot in the room (minus Robin) dropped what they were doing (literally) and rushed to protect Fleur.

"Look at the little fellow go!" cheered Robin as the ferret scurried across Fleur Pickles' body in a blur of fur while the robots tried in vain to catch him.

Then I noticed that Ali, Jess and Ivana were all free and had opened the cupboard. My plan had actually worked! Sort of.

Finally Fleur Pickles saw what was happening and shouted at the robots to get us, but it was too late – the Guardians had stopped, frozen in mid-lunge.

I looked over and saw Grandma standing by the computer in the corner.

"You did it!"

"No, you did," said Grandma. "All of you."

Fleur Pickles was shaking the robots. "What have you done to them?" she howled, then turned and started hammering the computer keyboard.

The Guardians' eyes were flashing and the smell of burning plastic had replaced Wee Freddie's stink.

"DEACTIVATION SEQUENCE INITIATED," they said in unison. "SELF-

DESTRUCT IN FIVE ..."

"NO!" said Fleur.

"FOUR ..."

"STOP!"

"THREE ..."

She tapped frantically at the keys. "Abort, you stupid thing! ABORT!"

"TWO ..."

"ONE."

I braced myself for the *BOOM!* But there was just an eerie silence and the light dimmed as four pairs of blue eyes flickered and then went dark.

"No bad for a bunch of weans, a wee dog, two auld women and a ferret, eh?" said Granny Anderson. "I always say – underestimate youngsters at your peril!"

Fleur Pickles glared at the old lady. "You think you've won," she hissed, "but this isn't over!" She made a grab for Robin's head, but Digby and Wee Freddie got there first.

Jess reached over and pulled out the wires, then picked Robin up.

"I believe the rest of me should be around here somewhere," said the robot.

"We found you!" called Ali, helping Ivana carry Robin's body from the cupboard.

Fleur Pickles pointed a shaking finger at the head. "I'm coming for you, ROBOT!" she snarled. "There's something special about you and I want it. And Fleur Pickles always gets what she wants in the end. You'll see!"

"Aye, well best a luck wi' that, hen," said
Granny Anderson. "We'll show ourselves oot."

ALL THE BETTER
TO SEE YOU WITH

I could see the audience from behind the
cardboard tree, rows of faces watching the
stage. I swallowed and checked the back of
my hand, but it was blank. Granny Anderson
had convinced me I didn't need a reminder any
more. I wasn't so sure.

Robin's voice boomed over the speakers as
the First Rabbit hopped out in front of Red
Riding Hood.

"Don't go to the cottage, Red!" he warned
her.

"There's danger up ahead!" sang the Second Rabbit.

"Don't go to the cottage, Red!" they chorused, then looked at me.

I shuffled out into the glaring spotlight. "That's not Grandma in bed!" I sang. *It's a robot – left by TV Celebrity Fleur Pickles. She kidnapped our grandma and forced her to build an army of scary robots to take over the world, but we stopped her!*

The audience gasped.

At least they would have done if I'd actually said that out loud! But I didn't. It was our secret and it had to stay that way.

It had been a mad dash to get back from the Pickle Factory and reattach Robin's head, then get to school in time for the performance. Granny Anderson wanted to get Robin and Grandma out of town as soon as possible, but the robot insisted on staying to do the play first. I was worried Fleur Pickles would come crashing into the hall, flanked by an army of robots, even though Grandma assured us that her virus had destroyed them all.

We didn't tell Mum and Dad everything that had happened – just that Fleur Pickles had found out that Robin was a robot, and so Grandma thought it might be a good idea if they *disappeared* for a while.

"You'll both be too big for a babysitter soon anyway," Dad had said, trying to make us feel better.

He was right, but Robin was more than our babysitter now. He was part of the family. We were all going to miss him. Especially Digby.

The play had finished and we were in the school car park, standing next to the shed-on-wheels, saying goodbye. The dog knew something was happening and was watching Robin with big, sad eyes.

"It won't be the same at home without you," I told the robot.

Robin gave me a hug, which was a bit like hugging a postbox, but nice all the same.

"It's most confusing," said

the robot, stroking his beard. "When I think about leaving, it feels as though some of my parts are missing, but I've checked and everything is in place."

Grandma put a hand on his shoulder. "That's how it feels when you miss the people you love," she told him. "Fleur Pickles was right about one thing – there's definitely something special about you!"

"That kilt for a start!" said Jess.

"If I am going to live in Scotland, I need to dress appropriately," the robot explained.

"Not everyone in Scotland wears a kilt."

"I think it suits him," said Granny Anderson. "I did warn him that wearin' a kilt on a motorbike would be a wee bit draughty round the nether regions. But I suppose wi' him being made of metal and that, he won't notice!"

"Nether regions?" said Ali. "Is that the part of Scotland where you live?"

"Not exactly," said Mum, stifling a laugh.

"I've heard Scotland is very beautiful." Ivana managed a sad smile.

"That it is!" said Granny Anderson. "Why not come and see for yourselves? It's no long 'til the holidays. You'd be welcome to spend them wi' us!"

I wondered what it would be like staying with Granny Anderson.

Ali was convinced she was some kind of government agent from the *Granny Spy Division*.

"Think about it," he'd said. "It's the perfect cover! Who's going to suspect an old lady?"

And people said *I* had a wild imagination! All the same, I had a feeling that a visit to Scotland would be … interesting, to say the least.

"Right," said Granny Anderson, winding Wee Freddie round her neck. "Time we got this wagon train a-rollin'." She climbed on to the motorbike and patted the seat behind her.

"On you get, metal man. Hold on tight now!"

Grandma waved from the sidecar as the ancient machine coughed into life, then rattled out through the gate. We stood on the kerb, waving through clouds of blue smoke until the shed-on-wheels was just tail lights and a distant rattle on the wind.

It was weird walking home without Robin. Digby was so miserable he barely stopped to sniff a single car tyre.

"Who's your project going to be about now?" I asked my sister, to take my mind off the empty feeling in my chest.

"Fleur Pickles," said Jess. "I'm not wasting thirteen full-colour pages and an exclusive interview. Ms Sternwood will definitely give me a gold star for that!"

"But—"

"I'm going to write about how Fleur Pickles has taught me that people aren't always what they appear to be, and that we can learn a lot from our mistakes."

"Sounds good," I said.

Jess narrowed her eyes as if she suspected I was being sarcastic, but I wasn't. I actually felt quite proud of her.

"I might do mine on Granny Anderson," I said.

"Ms Sternwood will think you made her up, but yeah, you should." Jess frowned. "By the way, you do know you're walking down the street – in public – dressed as a fluffy bunny rabbit, right?"

I shrugged. "Maybe I'm not what I appear to be either. I might look like a harmless bunny rabbit, but I just helped save the world!"

"Huh," said Jess.

We walked on in silence for a few moments.

"You still look like a dork," she said.

"At least I can change out of my costume… What are you going to do?"

THE END

Until next time, when I get the feeling that we might all be taking a trip to a secret location somewhere in the nether regions of Scotland...

ACKNOWLEDGEMENTS

Writing is a solitary task, but turning that story into a book requires a whole team of talented people. I would like to thank everyone involved in producing the book you are holding, especially Ruth and the dedicated team at Stripes and Little Tiger.

Special thanks to my editor Mattie, who has been with me every step of the way, and Cata whose superb drawings bring the characters to life in a way I never imagined possible. For their attention to detail (and laughing at my jokes!) appreciation to Jane and Susila for their copy-edit skills on the series. To Pip and her design team – respect and gratitude for turning our collection of words and pictures into a proper book!

Granny Anderson makes her first appearance in this story and has become one of my favourite characters. The twins' great-gran has lived all her life in a remote part of Scotland, and uses bits of local dialect and sayings when she speaks. I owe a huge debt of gratitude (and a giant box of chocolates) to Moira Foster, Elaine Hallyburton and Zan Phee for their advice on Granny Anderson's dialogue.

As always, a huge shout out and thanks to the thousands of librarians, teachers, parents, grandparents, booksellers, journalists and bloggers out there who do so much to make books available and exciting to readers. You ROCK!

Finally, love and thanks to my family and friends for their patience and support. Oh, and the shed's great, by the way – thanks!

THE ADVENTURES WILL CONTINUE IN...

MY ROBOT'S GONE WILD

COMING SOON!

Jake and Jess are on their way to Scotland
to visit Robin, who's been hiding out near a
remote loch with Grandma. Jake can't wait
to see his favourite robot but is shocked by
how much he's changed. Robin now spends
most of his time camouflaged in bushes and
can light a fire with a click of his fingers –
he's gone wild!

But when Grandma ropes the trio into a
plan to catch a local gang of thieves in the
act, it looks like Robin's new skills might just
save the day…

ABOUT THE AUTHOR

Abandoning childhood plans to be an astronaut –
or Batman – Dave Cousins went to art college in
Bradford, joined a band and was nearly famous.
His writing career began aged ten, drawing comics
and penning lyrics for an imaginary pop group.
Dave says that reading and writing stories helped him
along the bumpy path to growing-up, and hopes that his
books will play a similar role for today's readers.

When not scribbling stories and pictures,
Dave tours extensively. His events have been
described as "stand-up with books", or as
one reader put it: "well funny!" Dave has three
grown-up children and lives on a rock by the sea
in Wales, with his wife and a grumpy cat.

www.davecousins.net

ABOUT THE ILLUSTRATOR

Born in Bogotá, Colombia,
Catalina Echeverri lives in London with her
Northern Irish husband, Will, and their little daughter S.

Before settling in the UK Catalina spent time in Italy,
studying graphic design and eating pizza and ice cream
every day that she could. When she'd eaten it all, she
moved to Cambridge to study children's book illustration.
She has worked in children's publishing ever since, creating
books such as *Milo's Dog Says Moo*,
There's a Dinosaur in my Bathtub and *Lion and Mouse*.

Catalina is never without her sketchbook.
She particularly enjoys working on projects that
make a positive impact on people's lives.

www.cataverri.com

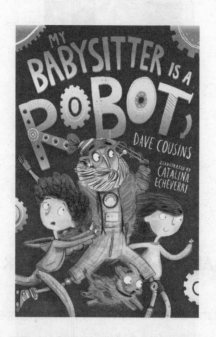